Have you ever felt two differe
like someone but you're angry
someone but they make you la
all mixed-up! Well, one day we ~~~~~ ~~~~~ up a word
in the dictionary and we came across a drawing of a
chimera. It was, the dictionary said, a mythical beast
with the head of a lion, the body of a goat and the tail
of a serpent. How mixed-up would that creature feel?
And what's more, no one even agrees on how to say
the poor thing's name! We say kim-era but some say
shi-mmera. What would you say?

And what would happen, we wondered, if Tashi met
such a mixed-up monster? Of course, we knew why a
Chimera might appear in Tashi's village – Wise-as-an-Owl
is having a lot of trouble leading his son Much-to-Learn
through the Book of Spells. His young pupil always wants
to bound ahead. And see what happens now: Tashi and
his friends are facing a terrible mixed-up monster whose
roars are filling the sky. We even frightened ourselves –
but we had fun doing it! How mixed-up is that?

ANNA AND BARBARA FIENBERG

Anna and Barbara Fienberg write the Tashi stories together, making up all kinds of daredevil adventures and tricky characters for him to face. Lucky he's such a clever Tashi.

Kim Gamble is one of Australia's favourite illustrators for children. Together Kim and Anna have made such wonderful books as *The Magnificent Nose and Other Marvels*, *The Hottest Boy Who Ever Lived*, the *Tashi* series, the *Minton* picture books, *Joseph,* and a full colour picture book about their favourite adventurer, *There once was a boy called Tashi.*

First published in 2007

Allen & Unwin
83 Alexander Street
Crows Nest 2065
Australia
Phone: (61 2) 8425 0100
Fax: (61 2) 9906 2218
Email: info@allenandunwin.com
Web: www.allenandunwin.com

National Library of Australia
Cataloguing-in-Publication entry:

Fienberg, Anna.

Tashi and the mixed-up monster.
ISBN 978 1 74175 191 8.

1. Tashi (Ficticious character) – Juvenile fiction. 2. Monsters – Juvenile
fiction. I. Fienberg, Barbara. II. Gamble, Kim. III Title. (Series: Tashi; 14).

A823.3

Cover and series design by Sandra Nobes
Typeset in Sabon by Tou-Can Design
Printed in Australia by McPherson's Printing Group

10 9 8

Tashi

and the
MIXED-UP
MONSTER

written by
Anna Fienberg
and
Barbara Fienberg

illustrated by
Kim Gamble

ALLEN&UNWIN

'Do you ever remember your dreams?' asked Jack.

'Sometimes,' said Dad, 'when they're scary.'

'Me too,' agreed Jack. 'Take last night. I was being chased through the jungle by a monster with two heads – one was a lion and the other a goat. The lion-head kept roaring "*rip, tear, kill!*" and the goat-head kept saying "stop and smell the grass why don't you?"'

'Gosh. Which jungle was this? The
African or the Amazon?'

'Oh Dad, what does it *matter*?'

'Well there's completely different animal
life for a start. Take your typical Amazon
forest—'

'Did it catch you in the end?' put in
Mum.

'The monster? No. The two heads were
so busy arguing, it got kind of paralysed.
Then a python slid down from a tree and
strangled it.'

'Must have been the African jungle,' said
Dad, 'what with the python and all.'

'That's not true, pythons are
everywhere,' said Mum. 'We had one in
our back yard when I was a girl.'

Dad shuddered. 'You never mentioned *that* when I came to visit.'

'You know, Tashi had troubles with a mixed-up monster,' Jack said. 'He was telling me about it yesterday.'

'A*ha*, maybe that's why you had the dream!' said Mum. 'What happened? Go on, we want to know everything.'

'Well, see, it was like this. It was
a sunny Sunday afternoon and Tashi,
Ah Chu and Lotus Blossom were sprawled
on the grass behind Wise-as-an-Owl's
house. They'd just had a big lunch and
felt a bit sleepy – especially Ah Chu.'

'Ah, that one!' cried Dad. 'He'd eat the
bottom off a porcupine if it stood still for
long enough!'

'Yeah. Well, they could see Wise-as-an-Owl nodding over a book in his garden workshop, and his son, Much-to-Learn, puttering about behind him at a table. Ah Chu was yawning, almost asleep, when suddenly Tashi put his head to the ground. "Listen," he said, "can you hear something rumbling?"

'A second later, Wise-as-an-Owl burst out of the workshop. "Tashi, children, *run*! – no, it's too late. *Hide*!" He pulled them over to some thick bushes.

'"What is it?" Tashi asked.

'Wise-as-an-Owl groaned. "Oh dear, I should have seen it coming. Much-to-Learn has been reading ahead of his lessons in the Book of Spells. It seems he's found the chapter on how to create a Chimera."

'The three friends looked at each other anxiously. "What is a Chimera?"

'"It's a creature from the past – a fearsome, fire-breathing monster with the head of a lion, the body of a goat and the tail of a serpent."

'"Wah! How big is it?" Tashi wanted to know.

'Wise-as-an-Owl's voice quavered. "This one is almost as big as the workshop."

'Suddenly the workshop walls split
apart and the roof shot up in the air.
A huge snarling lion's head appeared
above the skyline.

'"Or maybe even a bit bigger," Wise-as-
an-Owl faltered.

'The head sent out a thunderous roar
that rolled out, echoing and re-echoing
across the fields.

'"Do you think Much-to-Learn got
away?" Tashi asked in a small voice.

'"No. I left him hiding under the table."
Wise-as-an-Owl's face quivered and his
eyes filled. "I don't know how long he can
stay out of sight." The old man's knees
suddenly folded beneath him and he sank
onto the grass. "Help me up, Tashi. I must
go back to my son."

'Tashi and Lotus Blossom put their arms
around him and looked at each other
fearfully over his head.

'"What can we do, Wise-as-an-Owl?"
Tashi asked. "How can we get rid of this
creature?"

'"I can't say for sure," Wise-as-an-Owl moaned. "There is a magic formula somewhere for dealing with the monster, but it's not the sort of thing you study every day. And I couldn't stop to take the Book of Spells before leaving."

'"No, of course not," Tashi agreed. "I wonder what a Chimera eats. Do you know, by any chance?"

'"Well, lions eat animals and people, and goats eat grass and cardboard," Wise-as-an-Owl sighed. "It will be one or the other, I suppose. Help me up, would you?"

'"That roar didn't sound like a grass-eater to me," Ah Chu gulped. "And it sounded hungry."

'"You can't go just yet, not while that…thing is there!" Tashi said.

'But Wise-as-an-Owl climbed back through the bushes. He had only taken two shaky steps when the shell of the workshop fell away and the Chimera rose to its full height, unfurling a pair of monstrous wings.

'"You didn't say anything about *wings*, Wise-as-an-Owl!" squeaked Lotus Blossom.

'"That's because they shouldn't be there," the old man sighed. "Much-to-Learn has got it all wrong again."

'They clutched each other as the Chimera tested its wings, and then flew out across the rice fields.

'"Do you think it will come back?" Ah Chu whimpered.

'"Yes, I think it will," Wise-as-an-Owl nodded. "This was its birth-place after all. But I must use this chance to bring my son out."

'"And get the Book of Spells," Tashi added. "I'll come with you."

'Ah Chu took a deep breath. "We'll wait here and keep watch."

'"To warn you if it comes back," Lotus Blossom promised.

14

'Tashi heard Much-to-Learn before he saw him amongst the splintered planks and shattered glass of the workshop. He was moaning and cursing, trying to wriggle out from under the broken table.

'"My son, thank the gods, you're *safe*!" cried Wise-as-an-Owl.

'While he lifted the wood away, Tashi searched for the Book of Spells, his ears pricked anxiously for the sound of flapping wings. He found the book under a pile of rubble, undamaged except for a sooty hoof print right over the page *Mixed-Up Monsters*.

'Wise-as-an-Owl was gently
examining his son. "*Ouch!*" Much-to-
Learn yelled as he tried to move his right
arm. It was broken; Tashi could see it
dangling and useless. But they had no time
for making slings, Ah Chu's urgent whistle
told them that. Much-to-Learn flung his
good arm around his father's neck and
they hobbled back to their hideaway.

16

'Two heartbeats later, the Chimera glided down to its birth-place amongst the ruins of the workshop.

'Safely back in the bushes, Wise-as-an-Owl flipped through the Book of Spells until he found the page he needed: *How to Destroy the Chimera*. Tashi tried to peep over his shoulder. It was too hard to read the ancient writing in the dusky light, so he turned to help Lotus Blossom. She was making Much-to-Learn as comfortable as she could with a sling and a splint.

'Soon the old man lifted his head. "Yes, it's quite straightforward. Once we get the ingredients from my library–"

'Ah Chu choked. "Go back down there, do you mean?"

'"Just give me a list," Tashi said quickly. "I know where all your potions and mixing bowls are kept, Wise-as-an-Owl. I'm quick and light – it will be easier for me to clamber over all that wreckage. Look," he went on, "it's nearly dark and the Chimera has been quiet for ages. I'll creep down and see if it's asleep."

'Tashi wished he felt as brave as he had sounded. A droning noise greeted him as he drew near. He thought his pounding heart would surely wake the Chimera as he felt his way over the smashed walls and windows. The monster slept, eyes closed, wings furled amongst the wreckage. Only its great tail lay slowly twitching, gleaming through the grass.

'Tashi tip-toed to the library in the main house where the moonlight poured through the windows, lighting up the shelves of beakers in its cold, eerie beam. Working silently, Tashi found the ingredients on his list, one by one, and put them into a large mixing bowl. He was almost finished when he heard something move behind him.

'He stood, terrified, his insides churning.
The sound came again, slithering towards
him across the floor. The hairs on the back
of his neck prickled. He looked down and
saw something glittering in the moonlight,
beside his heel. The tip of the monster's
tail!

'Tashi tried to slow his breath, to make
his hands still. Maybe the creature would
think he was a statue, or a piece of wood.
But the tail was sliding over his foot!

'He dug his toes into his boots. He imagined he was a tree, rooted to the ground. The serpent tail was heavy, like the weight of two men.

'Tashi was melting with fright. But the tail came to rest over his feet. Oh *please*, thought Tashi, *please stay asleep*! He counted to one hundred, and still the tail didn't move. Then slowly, smooth as honey dripping from a spoon, Tashi slid one foot then the other from under the tail.

'When he was free, Tashi bolted back
to the hideaway. Wise-as-an-Owl told him
they'd have to wait until it was light
before mixing the potion. They all tried
to get some rest but twigs and stones stuck
into their backs and Ah Chu's stomach
was grumbling like thunder. When the sun
finally came up Ah Chu said it looked like
a great fried egg and that made everyone
even hungrier.

'But it was time to get to work. Wise-as-an-Owl checked every item, asking Tashi to tick each ingredient as he added it to the bowl. Much-to-Learn sniffed, offended by his father's choice of helper. "*I* could have done that, better than young Tashi," he said, "only my arm–"

'"If you hadn't played the fool with the Book of Spells, we wouldn't have to do any of this," his father growled.

'He turned to Tashi. "We'll wait until the Chimera goes hunting for its next meal and then take this bowl to his den. We'll just have to keep our fingers crossed that he drinks it when he returns."

'Finally the Chimera woke and left to look for food. When he was out of sight Tashi, with Wise-as-an-Owl close behind, carried the bowl of precious mixture down to the ruins of the workshop. He was just deciding where to put it when the air was suddenly filled with the screams of a terrified pig.

'"Quick Tashi, let's go!" Wise-as-an-Owl swung round, twisting his ankle on a loose board. He staggered and fell, hitting his head on the edge of the table as he went crashing down.

'Tashi's breath stopped in his chest. The old man's face was still. Tashi tugged at his arm and called his name, but there was no response. He wasn't dead, was he? You couldn't die from a fall, could you?

'He tried to drag his old friend across
the rubble. Wise-as-an-Owl was frail and
thin, but now he seemed as heavy as a
sackful of bricks.

'And then, Tashi looked up to see the
Chimera flying across the fields towards
him. So this is it, he thought. This is how
I'm going to die.

'He felt a sharp shove in the middle of his back and Much-to-Learn said, "Quick, take my father's feet, Tashi. You two, whatever your names are–"

'"*LOTUS* BLOSSOM is my name!" said Lotus Blossom, "and this here is AH *CHU*, if you *don't* mind, and as if you *wouldn't* know our names, when we've both followed you into this death-trap, risking our very *lives* for a mistake *you*–"

'"Oh just get on with it," panted Much-to-Learn. He was dragging the workshop door across the floor with his left hand.

'"What are you doing with that?" asked Lotus Blossom. But then she said nothing more as she watched him lift the door and prop it up against a broken chair.

'"Bring him over here, quick, and hide!" cried Much-to-Learn.

'They ducked down behind the door just as the Chimera dropped to the ground. It looked around warily and moved over to sniff the bowl. Four pairs of eyes watched it without blinking.

'It slurped the potion.

'Out of the corner of his eye, Tashi noticed that Wise-as-an-Owl had lifted his head. The old man looked around, dazed, and rubbed his forehead.

'*CRASH!* The door suddenly banged down, *WHUMP!* on the floor.

'The Chimera sprang up with a snarl
and faced its enemies. It spread its wings
wide, scales glinting like fire, cutting like
glass. Its teeth were bared, its nostrils
flared in fury. It pawed the ground with
its terrible hoof and opened its mouth and
roared a thousand times louder than the
Magic Warning Bell.

'The children clapped their hands over their ears and squeezed their eyes shut, and still the grinding roar went on and on and on until...

'"Open your eyes. Look!" cried Tashi.

'"No, I can't!" wailed Ah Chu.

'As the Chimera sprang towards them, Tashi could suddenly see through it, to the chair behind. The fiery scales were growing dull, wavering in the air like puddles after rain. The dripping teeth were fading with every second. Something hot stung Tashi's cheek, leaving a small wet patch. And then, as the children all opened their eyes wide, the monster dissolved like a bubble in the air and there was nothing left to see, at all.

'"What? How?" Ah Chu was rubbing his eyes as if he couldn't believe them. The others just stood silently, feeling their hearts thumping.

'"Well done, Father. Brilliant! I knew you'd find the very potion we needed! Let's–"

'But you know, they never did hear what Much-to-Learn was going to suggest because there was suddenly a dreadful yelling and cursing coming from the field below. Wise-as-an-Owl tottered off to find out what it was.

'He came back with Mr Ping from the village. Much-to-Learn was still beaming. "Well, as I always say, all's well that ends well!"

'"Yes you always do, my son," Wise-as-an-Owl said dryly. "Perhaps you would like to explain that to Mr Ping. He says that someone has stolen his prize pig."

'Well,' said Dad, getting up to make
a cup of tea, 'it just goes to show you
should always listen to your father. Isn't
that right, Jack?'

'I suppose,' said Jack. 'Especially if your
father is as wise as an owl.'

'That's right,' said Dad happily.
'Absolutely right.'

GUILTY OR NOT?

'That's *so* not fair!' exploded Mum when Tashi finished telling her the story.

'What?' asked Dad, walking into the kitchen.

'Well,' said Tashi, 'it was like this. At school today, Arthur Trouble drew a rude picture on the board with chalk but Angus Figment got the blame for it–'

'That's ridiculous!' said Dad. 'Angus Figment – as *if!*'

'Yeah,' agreed Jack, 'but see, Angus came into the classroom with chalk on his hands. The teacher wouldn't listen when he explained he'd just been drawing up handball lines in the playground, plus he wouldn't even *know* how to draw a naked mermaid because he's much more interested in Ancient Egypt and, by the way, did she know that the priests used to pluck out every hair on their bodies, even their eyelashes?'

'It's true,' said Tashi. 'Angus is only interested in Egyptian mummies. He draws them all over his books, and people's arms. Although sometimes he draws jackal masks, which look quite spooky.'

'Well, anyway,' Mum turned to Jack, 'you said you actually *saw* Arthur Trouble drawing on the blackboard. Why didn't you go and tell?'

'It's not that simple. Arthur's already in so much trouble and he's got a mean temper, and anyway I don't like dobbing.'

'But it's not fair on Angus!' cried Mum.

'That's right,' said Tashi. 'Something like that happened to me once, over a ball game.'

'Really?' said Dad. 'What did you do? Wait a sec, I'll make the tea – oh boy, I'm just in the mood for a story!'

'Well,' Tashi started, when the water had boiled, 'one day Ah Chu and I were playing a game of Catch when our ball flew over a wall and into Soh Meen's courtyard. And there was a loud splash. *Wah!*

'We had to run then because this furious man came barrelling out of the house. It was Soh Meen, chasing us with his broomstick. "Who did that?" he shouted. "Who threw that ball into my fish pond and very likely killed my precious carp!"

'"We're very sorry, Soh Meen," Ah Chu called over his shoulder. "Tashi didn't mean to do it." I gave Ah Chu a dirty look and stopped running.'

'I would have given him more than a dirty look!' said Dad. 'I would–'

'You would have sat him down,' said Mum, 'and talked to him about what it means to be a friend, and sharing responsibility.'

'How did you *know*? You took the words right out of my mouth!' cried Dad.

'Well, I didn't have time for that unfortunately,' said Tashi, 'because Soh Meen was shaking his fist at me.

'"It was a bad mistake, Soh Meen," I said. "Could we come in and see if the carp are hurt?"

'Well, thank goodness the fish were swimming about quite happily, but still Soh Meen gave us each a good whack with his broomstick and refused to return our ball. Apart from a sore bottom, that was the end of the matter, I thought.

'Until the next day.

'When I went to the square the following morning a crowd was gathered there. They were listening to a loud and angry speaker. I knew that voice.

'Someone let me through and I moved up to the front while the voice raged on, shouting "And then I saw them. My beautiful golden carp, lying upturned, dead, in a pool of stinking oil!"

'The murmur of the crowd was like a wind whooshing through the rice paddies. My heart sank.

'"And there is the culprit!" Soh Meen roared, pointing right at me. "Yesterday he attacked my carp with a ball. Then last night he sneaked back and finished my poor fish off! He poured bad oil into my beautiful clean pond!"

'"I didn't! I didn't! The ball was an accident..."

'But it was no use, Soh Meen went on and on until people started to believe him. The next few days were terrible. Ah Chu tried to explain what had really happened but Soh Meen wouldn't let him be heard. I kept turning the question over in my mind. How do you prove that you *didn't* do something?'

'I know, I know!' Dad cried. 'By proving that someone else *did*.'

'That's exactly right. But that was the easy bit – finding the real fish-poisoner would be the hard part. So I made a list of all the people who had a grudge against Soh Meen. There were quite a few, actually, but that didn't prove anything. And then my mother poured a glass of lemonade for me and there, suddenly, was the answer. "I have to go and see Wise-as-an-Owl straight away," I told her.

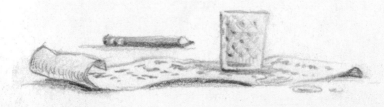

'Wise-as-an-Owl looked at me calmly
over his spectacles, just as he always does.
He said, "Sit down, Tashi, and get your
breath. Now, why do you need the Truth
Potion? You know I don't use these magic
brews without serious thought."

'When I explained my problem to him
he chuckled and shook his head. "I would
really like to be a cricket in the corner of
your kitchen tomorrow evening, Tashi. You
must be sure to tell me what happens
when they all find themselves speaking the
honest truth."

'So my family invited all the people on my list to come to our house that evening to discuss the situation. My mother told each one that their advice would be really important. Besides Soh Meen and his wife there were: the Wicked Baron, Mrs Ping, Mr Ping, Not Yet, Teacher Pang, Granny White Eyes, Tiki Pu and Luk Ahed.

'As soon as the guests arrived my mother poured them a glass of her delicious lemonade, which she had mixed up in a big jug, together with a cup and a half of Truth Potion.

'"This is very good," said the Baron, surprised, as he held out his glass for another helping.

'"It's the best I've ever had," agreed Mr Ping. "What's your secret?"

'"*I* know the secret of this lemonade," crowed Mrs Ping. "I peeked through the curtain one time while it was being made. They use limes as well as lemons, you know."

'My mother looked annoyed but Grandma poked me in the ribs and whispered, "It's working! Now we'll see what they *really* think about each other."

'My uncle Tiki Pu joined us at the table
and nodded to Luk Ahed. "You haven't
come along to our card evenings lately,
Luk Ahed."

'"No, and neither will any of the others
if you keep cheating like you did last time,
Tiki Pu," growled Luk Ahed.

'Before Tiki Pu could answer, Granny White Eyes said quietly to herself, "I wonder why the Baron always smells so unpleasant. He has plenty of money for hot water."

'The Baron went red and jumped to his feet, but my father quickly spoke up. "We were wondering if you would all be so kind as to tell us where you were on Saturday night? Someone might have seen or heard something that would help. Tiki Pu?"

'Tiki Pu shrugged. "I haven't been near Soh Meen's house for a week."

'My heart sank. Tiki Pu had been my surest suspect.

'Not Yet suddenly piped up. "Teacher Pang and I were in Soh Meen's garden that evening. We were keeping watch because we're sure he's the one who has been dumping his rubbish in other people's garbage bins. He's too mean to pay for a big enough bin for himself."

'Soh Meen choked on his lemonade.

'"But he didn't leave his house that night," Not Yet went on gloomily, "so it was a waste of time."

'"How dare you talk about me like that!" shouted Soh Meen.

'"No, I never would have dared to before," said Not Yet. "I don't know what came over me."

'Teacher Pang turned to the Baron.
"Did you see anything odd or unusual that
evening, Baron?"

'The Baron cleared his throat and was
surprised to hear himself say, "No, I was
at the other end of the village smashing
Mrs Yang's best melons. I am determined
to win the prize for the biggest melons at
this year's harvest festival, you see."

'Everyone gasped and looked at their hands, or the floor.

'"I didn't see anything either, I'm afraid," said Mrs Ping after an awkward pause. "I only went outside once during the evening because Mr Ping made the most dreadful smell and I had to get some fresh air."

'"I think he's just done it again," said Luk Ahed, who was sitting closest.

'"He thinks, just because they're silent, no one will notice," Mrs Ping said confidingly to Luk Ahed.

'"The silent ones are the worst," said Teacher Pang.

'"Well, I never knew that," said Mr Ping wonderingly. "You should have told me, dear. Next time we have beans, *I'll* be the one to step outside."

'Mrs Ping smiled and patted his hand across the table. "Thank you, Ping dear."

'There was a silence as everyone looked at the only person who hadn't explained where they'd been. "Well, *I* certainly didn't kill any fish," Luk Ahead said angrily.

'"No, I know you didn't. I did," whispered Mrs Soh Meen.

'"YOU!" thundered her husband.

'"Yes. It was all a terrible accident. I dug a hole at the bottom of the garden near the fish pond to get rid of some bad oil. It must have leaked into the pond overnight and killed the fish. It was wrong to let Tashi take the blame," she went on dreamily as the lemonade did its work, "but I knew I would never hear the end of it if I told my husband that it was *my* fault. He really is an awful bully. And Tashi, well, he doesn't have to *live* with him."

'No one spoke. Soh Meen cleared his throat and rubbed his nose.

'"It really is a strange smell. Perhaps it's bad breath," said Granny White Eyes, nodding at the Baron.

'"Or the terrible tobacco he smokes," Mrs Ping replied. "At least Mr Ping doesn't do that."

'"I'm not listening to any more of this," shouted the Baron as he stormed out of the house. "I was expecting a pleasant evening deciding about Tashi's punishment, not insults."

'My father thought he had better bring
the meeting to an end before anyone else
said something they would later regret, but
he didn't close the door quickly enough to
stop the Baron hearing Mrs Ping say to
Granny White Eyes, "That *was* an
interesting evening. Why don't we call in
on Mrs Yang and see if she knows what
happened to her melons?"

'Hmm,' said Jack, taking another cup-
cake. 'I wish we had a Truth Potion at our
school.'

Just then there was a knock at the door
and Angus Figment walked in. 'Guess what
everyone. Trouble confessed about the
mermaid!'

'How come?' asked Mum. 'Did you talk to him about what it means to be a friend and how he has to take responsibility?'

'Yeah, a bit, but you know how he's always pestering me to lend him my book *Secrets of the Tomb*? Well, I said he could have it for the weekend if he owned up. Plus I said I'd draw a really spooky jackal on him if he confessed straight away. So he did. You know, he's not so bad, Arthur Trouble, when you get to know him. May I have some cake, to go with the tea?' He shot a worried glance at Tashi. 'They're not Ghost Cakes or anything though, are they?'